D0399371

The Valentine's Day Mystery

Marion M. Markham

Illustrated by Karen A. Jerome

Houghton Mifflin Company

Boston 1992

Printed in the United States of America

BP 10 9 8 7 6 5 4 3 2 1

Library of Congress Cataloging-in-Publication Data

Markham, Marion M.
The Valentine's Day mystery / by Marion M. Markham : [illustrated by Karen A. Jerome].
p. cm.
Summary: On Valentine's Day twin detectives Kate and Mickey investigate a case involving a vanished garnet pin and a maestro of classical music.
ISBN 0-395-61589-5
[1. Valentine's Day — Fiction. 2. Twins — Fiction. 3. Sisters — Fiction. 4. Mystery and detective stories.] I. Jerome, Karen A., ill. II. Title.
PZ7.M33946Val 1992 92-8391
[Fic] — dc20 CIP
AC

Contents

1

Call the Police

"Hurry up," Mrs. Dixon called from the kitchen. "We don't want to be late." The twins stacked the valentines they had gotten in school and grabbed their coats.

Outside, it was snowing — the sort of wet snow that melts on your eyelashes and tickles the tip of your nose. Mrs. Dixon took off her glasses to wipe them dry.

Kate studied the shapes of the snowflakes on her mittens. She liked science and was curious about many things. Last week she had wondered why Billy Wade's Labrador retriever had eight black puppies and three that were gray with black spots. In the library, she read about something called a genetic code. The puppies' colors depended on what they inherited from both parents.

Mickey turned up her coat collar to keep the snow from dribbling down the back of her neck. The only codes she was interested in were for secret messages. She wanted to be a detective.

The Dixons were on their way next door to Miss Amanda Wink's house for a Valentine's Day party. Miss Wink's mother, Molly, opened the front door. She was short and round, and the twins had never seen her when she wasn't smiling.

"Come in, come in," she said. "Amanda is in the living room with Maestro Antonio-Corelli."

Behind her, Miss Wink's father, Horace, was licking his fingers. He looked fatter than he really was because he wore several sweaters. A red wool scarf circled his neck. Miss Wink's parents lived in Florida and Horace claimed he was always cold "up north."

"Frosting," he said, wiggling the fingers he was licking. "You girls get lots of valentines today?"

"Lots," Mickey said.

"And lots," added Kate.

Horace took their coats and hung them in the hall closet. "The ancient music man is already here," he said.

The man on the sofa next to Miss Wink was very thin. He didn't look ancient, though. His

hair and moustache — as black as the tuxedo he wore — didn't have even a sprinkling of gray. When he saw the Dixons, he stood. Miss Wink popped up, too.

"Maestro," she said, "these are my neighbors, the Dixons."

Mrs. Dixon held out her hand. Rather than shaking her hand, the man kissed it. "It is a privilege to meet Amanda's friends," he said.

"Maestro Antonio-Corelli has come to conduct the Ancient Music Society in a performance of his concerto." Miss Wink said the word "concerto" with breathless awe. Antonio-Corelli — who was two inches shorter than she was — smiled up at her.

Kate thought he looked too young to be a maestro. But then she didn't know what a maestro was. Something to do with being a famous musician, she guessed.

Mickey noticed that Miss Wink's lips were unnaturally pink. How strange. She didn't usually wear make-up.

Molly said, "Shall we have the cake now?"

The maestro smiled and offered his arm to Miss Wink. Together, they walked to the dining room.

Besides plates and forks, there was a very large cake on the table. It was frosted with pink icing. On top of the cake a heart-shaped cookie with red sprinkles sat on a big mound of frosting.

Kate said, "That cookie's just like the ones we had in school today."

"I baked the cake, but I bought the heart," Molly said. "A party cake should have some sort of decoration."

"Clever," Mickey said.

"Beautiful," Kate said.

Maestro Antonio-Corelli said, "Before the cake is cut, I wish to present Miss Amanda a gift." His accent was strange. So was the expression on his face when he reached inside his tuxedo.

"It's gone!" he said.

"What's gone?" asked Horace.

"The garnet pin for Amanda. Someone has stolen it from my pocket! Call the police!"

"A pin?" Horace sounded surprised.

"Oh, dear," said Miss Wink. Her face turned pale and Mickey was afraid she was going to faint.

"Take a deep breath, Amanda," her father ordered.

"When I remove my overcoat, I put pin from coat to tuxedo. Call the police — the gendarmes."

"Whoa," Horace said. "Let's not panic. We've got the best detectives in Springvale right here."

Antonio-Corelli looked very confused. "Detectives?" he said.

Mickey said, "He means us."

"Do not make the fun of me," Antonio-Corelli said. "The pin have belong to my dear, dead mother."

"Oh, dear," said Miss Wink again.

"It's got to be here somewhere," Molly said. "Let's look."

2

Finney and Huggins on the Job

Everyone except the maestro searched the living room. He sat on the sofa with his arms folded across his chest. He didn't move, except when Mrs. Dixon looked under the sofa cushions.

"*Mama mia, mama mia,*" he repeated over and over.

"A simple deduction tells me the maestro is Italian," Mickey whispered to Kate, as they crawled across the floor looking under furniture.

"Even I could deduce that," Kate whispered back. "But where's the garnet pin?"

Mickey said, "I don't know."

Horace Wink looked up the fireplace chimney. Molly Wink looked around the plants on the sill of the bay window. Miss Wink looked beneath everything on the table next to the sofa. She even lifted a colorful glass paperweight, although nothing could possibly have been under it.

The searchers moved back into the dining room. Nothing. Then they explored the front hall. Still nothing.

"Call the gendarmes," Antonio-Corelli said again.

"Yes, Maestro," Miss Wink said. She grabbed the telephone book. As if hoping to find the missing pin between its pages, she held it up and shook it. Then she dialed.

While they waited for the police, the hunt continued.

Mickey stopped looking and started thinking. The solution to this mystery wasn't going to be found under a paperweight. She heard a siren in the distance. It grew louder and louder, finally stopping in front of the house. Two policemen came to the front door.

The Dixons knew them. The short, fat policeman with a box of raisins in his hand was Officer Huggins. The tall, thin policeman with the smile was Officer Finney. The smile got bigger as he looked at Miss Wink.

"Good to see you again, Amanda, ma'am," he said.

"Finney and Huggins on the job," Officer Huggins said. The hand holding the raisin box jerked up in a sharp salute. Raisins showered the floor. He turned red and stuffed the box in his pocket.

"Does your dog like raisins?" he asked Horace.

Horace said, "We don't have a dog."

"How sad," said Officer Huggins. "Every family should have a pet."

Officer Finney said, "*You* don't have a dog."

"And I'm sad," said Officer Huggins. He gathered the spilled raisins and dropped them in his pocket.

The maestro stood. "Arrest these people," he demanded.

"All of them?" Officer Finney sounded surprised.

Antonio-Corelli thought about it. "One of them anyway."

"Which one?" Officer Huggins asked.

"It is for you to discover who stole my mother's jewels."

Officer Huggins took out a notebook and pencil. "Describe the missing property," he said.

"Round — a gold circle set with garnets. So big." The maestro made a circle with his thumb and forefinger. "It is my valentine gift to Miss Amanda."

Officer Huggins wrote in his notebook. Officer Finney only scowled. Then the two whispered between themselves.

Mickey said, "Of course, you're going to question everyone."

"Of course," Officer Huggins said. He turned toward the sofa where Miss Wink and her mother were now sitting.

"Separately," Mickey added.

"Naturally," Officer Finney said.

Kate said, "You might as well begin with us — in the dining room."

The maestro said, "I demand that one of the gendarmes stay here. To guard the front door."

Officer Finney said, "Who would we be guarding it against? You'll all be here watching each other."

"Sensible man," said Horace.

3

Questions, But No Answers

The policemen followed the twins into the dining room. Officer Huggins pushed the valentine cake to one side.

"We need to make a timetable of everyone's movements," Mickey said.

"Oh, we *do*?" Officer Huggins said. "Are you on the Springvale police force now?"

"We've helped you before," Kate reminded him.

Officer Finney said, "She's right."

Officer Huggins frowned. "The sergeant won't like it," he said. Then he added, "What are we looking for?" — and the twins knew they could stay and help.

Mickey said, "What everyone was doing between the time the maestro came and when we got here."

"Why?" Officer Finney asked.

Kate knew what her sister was thinking. "Antonio-Corelli and Miss Wink were sitting together on the sofa when we arrived. They walked to the dining room together. Unless Miss Wink took the pin, no one was close enough to get it out of his pocket."

"Motive and opportunity," Mickey said. "Those are the two important things. We don't have a motive, so we'll look for opportunity."

Officer Finney nodded. "Where do we start?" he asked.

"With the maestro," said Mickey.

Officer Huggins said, "Antonio-Corelli wouldn't steal something he already owned."

Mickey said, "You need to know where *he* was. Otherwise you won't know who had the opportunity."

Officer Finney brought Antonio-Corelli in. The maestro refused to sit.

"I don't see why you question me," he said. "*I* am not the criminal."

"So you have nothing to hide," Officer Finney said sharply.

"Of course, I have nothing to hide," the maestro said.

Officer Huggins said, "Motive and opportunity. Those are the important clues to solving a mystery."

Officer Finney said, "We'll compare your story with the others'. If someone is lying, we'll find out."

The maestro frowned at the twins. "Why are they here?"

Officer Finney said, "*We* ask the questions."

"What's your name, sir?" Officer Huggins said.

"Maestro Antonio-Corelli."

Officer Huggins wrote in his notebook. "Your address?" he asked.

"In Springvale, it is the Bayside Hotel."

Officer Finney said, "Where do you live when you're not in Springvale?"

"Milan."

"Italy?" said Officer Huggins.

"Of course, Italy." Again Officer Huggins made a note.

"What brought you to town?" Officer Finney asked.

"The Ancient Music Society is giving first performance of my concerto."

Mickey said, "I thought the Ancient Music Society played ancient music."

Antonio-Corelli explained, "My concerto is based on sixteenth-century themes."

Officer Huggins asked the value of the pin and Antonio-Corelli said it was priceless, because it had belonged to his dear mother.

"Value unknown," said Officer Huggins, as he wrote.

Officer Finney said, "When did you last see it?"

"In front hall — when I arrive."

"What time was that?" asked Officer Finney.

"The grandfather clock was striking the quarter hour, seven-fifteen. Mr. Wink took my overcoat."

Kate said, "But the party wasn't until eight." The maestro glared at her. He had blue eyes. And blond eyelashes. Strange, since his eyebrows were as black as the hair on his head. She wondered what color hair his parents had.

"You came early?" Officer Huggins said.

"I wanted to talk to Miss Amanda. Alone."

Officer Finney scowled again. "Then what?" he asked.

"I went to the living room with her father."

"What did you talk about?" Officer Finney asked. "When you were *alone.*" He put special emphasis on "alone."

"We were not alone. Her father go in and out. Then Mrs. Wink come from kitchen and stay until doorbell ring and these girls arrive with their mother."

"What time was that?"

"Just after eight, I think."

Officer Huggins looked toward Kate and she nodded.

"So you and Miss Wink stayed in the living room between seven-fifteen and eight o'clock?" asked Officer Finney.

"That's right." Without waiting for permission, Antonio-Corelli turned to leave.

Mickey said, "Were you on the couch the whole time?"

“*Si,*” Antonio-Corelli said.

As he left, Mickey noticed that his tuxedo pants were very shiny in back. The bottoms of the pants’ legs were frayed, too. No wonder he was giving Miss Wink his mother’s garnet pin. He probably couldn’t afford to *buy* her a present. But why give her anything at all? Most people just send cards for Valentine’s Day.

Could Antonio-Corelli be Miss Wink’s boyfriend? The idea seemed silly.

4

Miss Wink

Next, Officer Finney brought in Miss Wink. Her hand shook as she rested it on the table.

"I can't imagine what Carlos must think," she said.

"Carlos?" Officer Finney looked puzzled.

"Maestro Carlos Antonio-Corelli. With a hyphen."

"What's with a hyphen?" Officer Huggins asked.

"Antonio-Corelli. His name is Carlos Antonio-hyphen-Corelli."

Officer Huggins turned his notebook back a page and wrote something. Then he asked, "What's your name, ma'am?"

Miss Wink looked surprised. "You know my name," she said.

Officer Finney explained, "For the record. Regulation number six-seventy-three. I quote: 'Record full names and addresses of all witnesses to a crime.'"

"But I didn't witness the crime," said Miss Wink.

"We'll get to that later. Right now, we need your name."

"Amanda Wink. No hyphen."

Officer Huggins wrote that down. Then he asked, "Your address?"

"*This* address," Miss Wink said, in a tone that dared him to ask her what this address was. He didn't.

Instead he said, "How long have you known Antonio-hyphen-Corelli?"

"Seven days," she said.

Officer Finney said, "You've only known him for a week, yet you invited him to a valentine party?"

Miss Wink blushed. "The maestro and I share a mutual love," she said. "A love of music, particularly music of the sixteenth century."

"Tell us about the evening's events as you remember them," Officer Huggins asked.

"Carlos arrived early. I heard the doorbell and

then, a few seconds later, the clock struck the quarter hour. Seven-fifteen."

"Your father answered the door?" Officer Huggins asked. She nodded.

Officer Finney said, "Antonio-Corelli said that he had the pin in the front hall. Did you see it?"

"I didn't come downstairs right away."

Mickey asked, "How long were you upstairs? After he arrived, I mean."

"About five minutes. I, er . . ." Miss Wink blushed again. "I stopped to comb my hair and put on a little lipstick."

"What happened next?" Officer Finney asked.

"My father left and Carlos and I chatted."

"About seven-thirty?" Mickey asked.

Miss Wink looked confused. "Why would we talk about seven-thirty?"

"When your father left," Mickey said. "Was it about seven-thirty?"

"I suppose so."

"About what?" Officer Finney asked.

Now Officer Huggins looked confused. "What about what?" he said.

"What *did* they chat about?" Officer Finney said.

"Music," Miss Wink answered quickly.

Officer Huggins said, "Antonio-hyphen-Corelli said he wanted to see you alone. Do you know why?"

Miss Wink's blush spread down her throat, and Mickey noticed that even the backs of her hands turned pink.

"No," she said, her voice very low. The twins strained to hear her over the sound of snow blowing against the windows.

"Where was your mother?" Officer Finney asked.

"In the kitchen," Miss Wink said. "Frosting the cake."

Mickey said, "Antonio-Corelli told us your mother came into the living room and stayed until we got here."

Miss Wink thought for a moment. "I think she was there when my father went out back for wood to start a fire."

"What time was that?" asked Mickey.

"I don't know. Just before you came." Her lower lip quivered. "I've never been very good about time." She stared at the heart cookie on the cake.

Officer Finney patted Miss Wink's shoulder. "Don't be upset, Amanda. No one expects you to remember everything."

5
Horace

Horace Wink was next. With a dramatic gesture, he swung his scarf over his shoulder so that both ends hung down in back. Like the maestro, he seemed to prefer standing.

"Are you cold?" asked Officer Finney.

"I've been cold ever since I arrived," he said. He walked over to a coffeepot on the sideboard. "Coffee anyone?" he asked, pouring himself a cup. No one else wanted any.

"Your name," Officer Huggins asked.

"Horace Wink."

"Address?"

"Here, temporarily."

"When you're not here?"

"Seventeen-oh-one Palmdale Court. Citrus Beach, Florida. Three, two, four —"

"We don't need your zip code," Officer Huggins said. "Not unless you're going back to Florida before we solve the crime."

"I'm not going back to Florida until our house is built."

Officer Finney said, "How can you have an address if you don't have a house?"

"We had a house," said Horace. "It burned down. A tiny flaw in one of my inventions."

"I didn't know you were an inventor," Kate said. Inventing was a little like science.

"I invented a clock with tiny mice that ran up a cord — one for each hour. At midnight the mice started down the cord again. My Hickory Dickory Dock Clock."

"Oh," said Kate. A Hickory Dickory Dock Clock didn't sound very scientific.

Horace said, "Can we hurry this up? Amanda's party has already been ruined by that musician."

Mickey thought that it wasn't the maestro who had ruined things.

"Amanda didn't want a party," he said. "She thinks she's too old to celebrate Valentine's Day. I told her that getting old is popular these days. I'm seventy-nine and proud of it."

Horace sipped his coffee. "You have to keep up

with the times. I wasn't a bit sorry to see buses replace the trolley cars, even though I lost my job

as a conductor. You can't stand in the way of progress."

"You were a trolley car conductor?" Mickey asked.

"First and last job I ever had. A good job, too. Punching tickets gave me lots of time to concentrate on my inventions."

Officer Finney said, "We're trying to find out exactly where everyone was when the pin was stolen."

"You know *when* it was taken?" Horace looked surprised.

"Not exactly. But it disappeared sometime between seven-fifteen and eight o'clock. Where were you during that time?"

"All over everywhere," Horace said.

Kate hid a giggle. "Everywhere" meant "all over." Mother called that a redundancy — using two words that meant the same thing. Like saying pizza pie, when "pizza" meant "pie." Horace was a very redundant person. Too much of everything — like the sweaters. And the muffler. This house was warm enough, even for a man who lived in Florida.

Officer Huggins said, "No one can be everywhere at the same time."

"I meant I don't know where I was every minute."

Officer Finney said, "Just tell us what you did, Mr. Wink."

Horace looked up at the ceiling as if he was trying to remember. "Well," he said slowly. "Right after dinner I was in the living room inventing."

"You're an inventor?" Officer Huggins said.

"Didn't I just say so?"

"I know," said Officer Huggins. "But I didn't write it down before. I didn't know it was important to our investigation."

Mickey couldn't see how it was important now. Nothing they had learned so far seemed to get them any closer to solving the mystery.

"I was thinking about an invention when the doorbell rang. At seven-fourteen-and-a-half."

"How can you be so precise?" asked Officer Finney.

"Because I got up to answer

the door. And that Antonio-Corelli fellow came in. As he was taking off his coat, the clock struck seven-fifteen."

Kate thought that seven-fifteen was one thing everyone agreed on.

Officer Finney asked Horace if he had seen the pin, and he said no.

"Mr. Antonio-hyphen-Corelli said that he moved it from his overcoat to his tuxedo," Officer Huggins said.

"I didn't notice," Horace said. "I was thinking about my new invention." He leaned forward and one end of the scarf flopped down. "Matter of fact, I told him about it — automatically adjusting suspenders. Either of you fellows wear suspenders to hold up your pants?"

The policemen shook their heads.

Officer Finney said, "They're against regulations."

Kate sighed. Horace was definitely more eccentric than scientific. No wonder Miss Wink was strange sometimes. She had inherited that from her father. She got her friendly smile from her mother.

"I was telling the maestro about the suspenders

when Amanda came downstairs," Horace said.

Mickey asked, "Then what did you do?"

Horace took a moment to answer. "I think that's when I set the dining room table."

"How long were you in there?" Officer Finney asked.

"In and out and then in again, you mean," Horace said. "I couldn't find the tablecloth. And there weren't enough clean forks, so I started the dishwasher."

"Mr. Antonio-Corelli said you returned to the living room several times."

"To tell the truth, I was watching him. There's something funny about that fellow. Shifty eyes."

Kate said, "There *is* something odd about the maestro. He dyes his hair."

"How do you know?" Officer Finney asked.

"His eyelashes are blond."

"Lots of people dye their hair," Officer Huggins said. His hand unconsciously went to his own head.

"But why would someone with blue eyes and blond eyelashes dye it black?" Kate said. "Light brown would look more natural."

Horace said, "He probably wants to marry Amanda for her money."

"Miss Wink is rich?" Mickey was surprised.

"Not rich. Comfortable. She gets the money from an oil-refining process I invented."

Kate said, "You invented a new process for refining crude oil?" An oil-refining process *had* to be scientific.

"Sunflower oil," Horace said. "For cooking. She foolishly told the maestro about it."

"I noticed Antonio-Corelli's tuxedo was frayed," Mickey said. "As if it's old and he can't afford a new one."

Horace started to say something, but Officer Finney interrupted. "Can we get back to why we're here. Amanda — ah — Miss Wink said that her mother came into the living room after she finished icing the cake."

"That's right. I was loading the dishwasher. I sent Molly to keep an eye on things."

Suddenly Mickey had a thought. "Maybe there is no garnet pin," she said.

The men looked at her.

"Maybe he made it up."

Officer Finney said, "Why would he do that?"

"It's Valentine's Day. If Mr. Wink is right about his wanting to marry Miss Wink, he might have thought he should give her a present. Only he didn't have money to buy one."

Officer Huggins said, "Then why would he want the police?"

"To back up his story," Mickey explained. "Even if you didn't find the pin, Miss Wink would believe there was one."

Kate said, "Remember how he wanted to know why you were asking *him* questions?"

"That's right," Officer Finney said. "I even asked him if he had anything to hide."

Kate had an idea, too. "I'd like to see his passport," she said.

Horace said, "Now why didn't I think of that," and dashed from the room, his red scarf flapping behind him.

6
The Maestro

The others followed. Officers Finney and Huggins got to the door at the same time. For a second they got stuck in it.

In the living room, Miss Wink sat on the couch between the maestro and Mrs. Dixon. Nervously, her hands twisted a handkerchief.

"Where's your passport?" Horace demanded.

The maestro jumped up. "I am not the criminal," he said.

"Then show us your passport."

"I — I don't have it. I left it at my hotel."

Kate said, "A passport is very valuable. You shouldn't leave it around."

"It is in the hotel safe," Antonio-Corelli said.

Officer Finney said, "Call and ask them to take it *out* of the safe." The maestro turned pale.

"Carlos. What's wrong?" Miss Wink asked. He sank down on the sofa again.

"I — ah — it's hot in here."

Horace said, "This house hasn't been hot for two months."

Kate said, "You don't have a passport, do you?"

The maestro shook his head.

"An illegal alien," Officer Finney shouted.

Miss Wink gasped and twisted her handkerchief so hard that Mickey was afraid it would tear. Officer Huggins pulled handcuffs from his pocket, spilling raisins again.

Kate said, "I don't think he's Italian at all."

"Of course not," said Mickey. "Italians don't call the police gendarmes. That's French."

Miss Wink looked at him. "Is this true, Carlos?"

The maestro said, "I was born in Milan." He sounded firm. Then he looked at the handcuffs in Officer Huggins's hand. "Milan, Tennessee; not Italy. No one will play sixteenth-century music by an American composer named Carlson."

Mickey said, "There wasn't any pin, was there?"

"Yes, there was," he said firmly. "I bought it this afternoon and the sales slip is still in my pocket."

Miss Wink said, "You told us that it had belonged to your mother." Her voice trembled and she looked as if she would cry. Mrs. Dixon reached over and grabbed her hand.

"The pin was in a small white jewelry box in my pocket."

Kate said, "You never mentioned anything about a box."

Antonio-hyphen-Corelli Carlson said, "I didn't care about the box. It was the pin I wanted to find."

Mrs. Dixon said, "How could we find it if we didn't know it was in a box?"

While her mother was talking, Mickey was thinking. She thought she knew who the thief was.

Turning to Horace, she said, "Miss Wink said that you went out to get wood for the fireplace. But there's no fire."

"I told you," Horace said. "While Amanda and this fellow were in the living room, I was loading the dishwasher."

"Horace," Molly said, "you know I did the dishes right after dinner. I'm not a housekeeper who lets things pile up."

Kate said, "Instead of getting wood *or* loading the dishwasher, you were hiding the box somewhere."

"Not somewhere," Mickey said. "In the dining room. It's just like the Edgar Allan Poe story, 'The Purloined Letter.' The box is in plain sight." She

paused dramatically. "Underneath the red cookie on the cake."

Officer Huggins hurried back to the dining room.

"Not exactly in plain sight," said Horace. "I smeared frosting on it."

Mickey said, "That's why you were licking your fingers when we arrived."

Now Miss Wink did begin to cry. "Oh, Papa. Why would you do it?"

"When I saw him take the box from his overcoat pocket, I thought he had a ring in it — an engagement ring for you. I didn't want you marrying some phony foreigner."

"You didn't know he wasn't Italian," she said.

"I knew he wasn't good enough for my daughter."

"To you, no one has ever been good enough for me."

Officer Huggins returned with the box. Frosting was smeared on his hands and uniform. "Is this it?"

The maestro looked inside the box and nodded. Officer Huggins turned to Horace.

"How did you expect to get away with it?" he asked.

"Get away with what?" Horace said. "I didn't plan to 'get away' with anything. I just wanted the box to disappear until he left town. Then I'd pretend I had found it and return it to him."

Mrs. Dixon said, "But surely we'd find it when we cut the cake."

Horace looked at his wife. "Not when Molly made a cake big enough to feed an army." He turned to Officer Finney. "She always overdoes things."

"Do you still want us to arrest someone?" Officer Finney asked the maestro.

The maestro shook his head. "No. But I would like to know how he got it without my knowing."

Horace said, "I wasn't inventing every minute that I was a trolley car conductor. I also watched for pickpocket thieves."

Was that a redundancy? Kate wasn't sure. Pickpockets *were* thieves. But not all thieves were pickpockets.

"It didn't take long to learn how they did it. I practiced on the pickpockets themselves. When I saw one put someone else's wallet in his own pocket, I'd lift it from him and pretend I'd found it on the floor. Then I would give it back to the

real owner." Horace was obviously proud of himself.

"You should have turned the pickpockets over to the police," Officer Huggins said.

"And lose time in court, away from my inventing? Never."

Mickey said, "Maybe you should invent a pick-proof pocket."

"Say, that's an idea."

Molly said, "Not until after Amanda has her Valentine's Day party." She turned to the policemen. "Can you stay?"

Officer Huggins said, "We'd love to."

"Definitely," said Officer Finney. He took Miss Wink's hand and led her toward the dining room.

"Now *he's* good enough for her," Horace whispered to the twins, as he wrapped his red scarf one more loop around his neck.

None of them realized the maestro had left until they felt the cold draft from the front door.